To Nana, Papa, GrandJan, Granddaddy, Grandpa Hart, and all the grandparents who hold us in their strong arms, and to Ava Rose, Ricky, Maria, and Rich, my wishes come true.—M.C.L.

For Ayumi. —S.I.

PHILOMEL BOOKS
A division of Penguin Young Readers Group.
Published by The Penguin Group.
Penguin Group (USA) Inc., 375 Hudson Street, New York, NY 10014, U.S.A.
Penguin Group (Canada), 90 Eglinton Avenue East, Suite 700, Toronto, Ontario M4P 2Y3, Canada
(a division of Pearson Penguin Canada Inc.).
Penguin Books Ltd, 80 Strand, London WC2R 0RL, England.
Penguin Ireland, 25 St. Stephen's Green, Dublin 2, Ireland (a division of Penguin Books Ltd).
Penguin Group (Australia), 250 Camberwell Road, Camberwell, Victoria 3124, Australia
(a division of Pearson Australia Group Pty Ltd).
Penguin Books India Pvt Ltd, 11 Community Centre, Panchsheel Park, New Delhi - 110 017, India.
Penguin Group (NZ), 67 Apollo Drive, Rosedale, North Shore 0632, New Zealand (a division of Pearson New Zealand Ltd).
Penguin Books (South Africa) (Pty) Ltd, 24 Sturdee Avenue, Rosebank, Johannesburg 2196, South Africa.
Penguin Books Ltd, Registered Offices: 80 Strand, London WC2R 0RL, England.

Published simultaneously in Canada. Manufactured in China by South China Printing Co. Ltd.
Design by Gunta Alexander and Katrina Damkoehler. Text set in Post Mediaeval.
The illustrations were painted in watercolor on Fabriano paper.
Library of Congress Cataloging-in-Publication Data
Cusimano, Maryann K.
You are my wish / Maryann Cusimano Love ; illustrated by Satomi Ichikawa.   p. cm.
Summary: Illustrations and rhyming text describe how a grandparent and child complement one another.
[1. Stories in rhyme. 2. Grandparent and child—Fiction.] I. Ichikawa, Satomi, ill. II. Title.
PZ8.3.C965Ys 2010   [E]—dc22   2009009557
ISBN 978-0-399-24752-1
1 3 5 7 9 10 8 6 4 2

You Are My WISH

Maryann Cusimano Love

illustrated by Satomi Ichikawa

Philomel Books • Penguin Young Readers Group

I am your grandparent;

you are my grandchild.

I am your wise face;

you are my new-tooth smile.

I am your silver hair;

you are my curlyhead.

I am your favorite quilt;

you are my springy bed.

I am your buttons;

you are my ticklish belly.

I am your home-baked bread;

you are my grape jelly.

I am your garden;

you are my daisy chain.

I am your strong arms;

you are my fast airplane.

I am your fountain;

  you are my splish.

    I am your penny;

      you are my wish.

I am your fishing line;

you are my squirmy bait.

I am your patient gaze;

you are my just-can't-wait.

I am your slow steps;

you are my hurry up.

I am your horsey;

you are my giddyup.

I am your family tree;

you are my rope swinging.

I am your old guitar;

you are my loud singing.

I am your soft lap;

you are my climb.

I am your story;

you are my rhyme.

I am your rocking chair;

    you are my snuggled deep.

I am your good-night prayer;
you are my fast asleep.